WELCOME TO
PASSPORT TO READING
A beginning reader's ticket to a brand-new world!

Every book in this program is designed to build read-along and read-alone skills, level by level, through engaging and enriching stories. As the reader turns each page, he or she will become more confident with new vocabulary, sight words, and comprehension.

These PASSPORT TO READING levels will help you choose the perfect book for every reader.

READING TOGETHER
Read short words in simple sentence structures together to begin a reader's journey.

READING OUT LOUD
Encourage developing readers to sound out words in more complex stories with simple vocabulary.

READING INDEPENDENTLY
Newly independent readers gain confidence reading more complex sentences with higher word counts.

READY TO READ MORE
Readers prepare for chapter books with fewer illustrations and longer paragraphs.

This book features sight words from the educator-supported Dolch Sight Words List. This encourages the reader to recognize commonly used vocabulary words, increasing reading speed and fluency.

For more information, please visit passporttoreadingbooks.com.

Enjoy the journey!

ISBN 978-0-545-79594-4

12 11 10 9 8 7 6 5 4 3 2 1   14 15 16 17 18 19/0

Printed in the U.S.A.   40

First Scholastic printing, September 2014

Cover design by Phil Caminiti

DINOTRUX
GO TO SCHOOL

CHRIS GALL

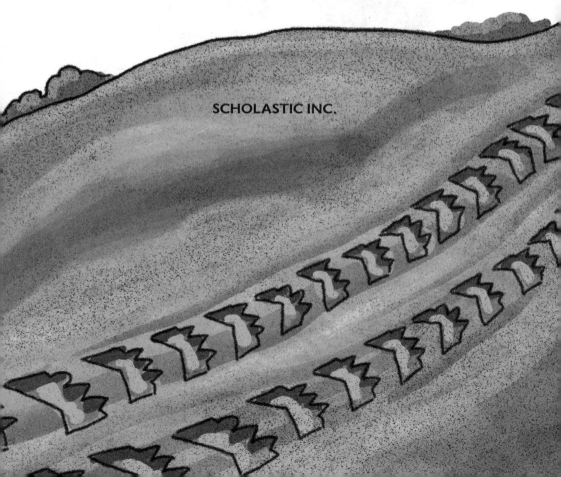

SCHOLASTIC INC.

GUIDE TO THE DINOTRUX

CEMENTOSAURUS
seh · men · toh · SOR · us

CRANEOSAURUS
cray · nee · oh · SOR · us

DELIVERADON
deh · LI · ver · uh · don

DIGASAURUS
dig · uh · SOR · us

DUMPLODUCUS
dump · luh · DUH · kus

DOZERATOPS
doh · ZAIR · uh · tops

GARBAGEADON

gar • BAJ • uh • don

ROLLODON

ROHL • oh • don

SEMISAURUS

sem • ee • SOR • us

SEPTISAURUS

sep • ti • SOR • us

TANKERSAURUS

tank • er • SOR • us

TOWADON

TOH • uh • don

TYRANNOSAURUS TRUX

ty • RAN • oh • sor • us   TRUKS

The Dinotrux woke up.

The sun was shining.

But summer was over.

It was the first day of school.

"I do not want to go to school,"
said Dumploducus.

"We will go together," said Craneosaurus.
Craneosaurus lifted Dumploducus
out of bed.

The Semisaurs rumbled by.

"Do not be late! Do not be late!" they said.

Dozeratops pushed boulders out of the way.
"I will clear our path to school," he said.

"This year, we will have much to learn,"
Craneosaurus said. "We will need books."
He loaded Dumploducus with books.

The books were very heavy.

Dumploducus could barely move his tires.

"I will tow you to school," said Towadon.

Rollodon rolled up.

"We will need supplies," he said.

He rolled on top of some logs.

He rolled and rolled until the logs were flat.

"Now we have lots of paper!" he cried.

Garbageadon heard his stomach growl.

"What if there is not enough food

for lunch?" he said.

"What if I run out of gas?"

"I will bring extra food for you,"
said Deliveradon.

Tyrannosaurus Trux was worried.

"I hope our teacher is not a giant, smelly caveman," he said.

Digasaurus drew a picture in the dirt.

"Like this?" said Digasaurus.

Tyrannosaurus Trux laughed.

"Yes! If he is scary, I will show him my teeth!"

Cementosaurus was upset.

"Is there a bathroom at school?"

he asked.

"Of course," said Garbageadon.

"I have to go all the time,"
said Cementosaurus.
"I know. Just raise your hand like
this," said Garbageadon.

"Will we have juice?" cried Septisaurus.

"I will fill my tank with juice
for everyone," said Tankersaurus.

"Thank you, Tankersaurus.

I need lots of juice!" Septisaurus said.

He let out a sigh of relief.

The Dinotrux arrived at school.

Garbageadon found the garbage can.

Dozeratops moved the desks to make room.

Digasaurus drew on the chalkboard.

Tyrannosaurus Trux found a new box
of pencils.

Then he chomped the box in half.

"Now there will be enough for all of us!"

he roared.

The teacher came into the classroom.

He was a giant, smelly caveman.

He was carrying three big clubs.

The Dinotrux trembled in fear.

"It is not possible!" shouted Digasaurus.

"He looks just like my drawing!"

The bell rang.

The teacher started to juggle.

The Dinotrux laughed.

School was not so scary after all.

They were together with friends.

And it would soon be time for recess!